DISNEY
THE LION GUARD

BUNGA THE WISE

ADAPTED BY Steve Behling

BASED ON THE EPISODE WRITTEN BY John Loy

FOR THE SERIES DEVELOPED FOR TELEVISION BY Ford Riley

ILLUSTRATED BY Premise Entertainment

DISNEY PRESS
Los Angeles · New York

Copyright © 2016 Disney Enterprises, Inc. All rights reserved. Published by Disney Press, an imprint of Disney Book Group. No part of this book may be reproduced or transmitted in any form or by any means, electronic or mechanical, including photocopying, recording, or by any information storage and retrieval system, without written permission from the publisher. For information address Disney Press, 1101 Flower Street, Glendale, California 91201.

First Paperback Edition, January 2016 10 9 8 7 6 5 4 3
ISBN 978-1-4847-1967-1
FAC-029261-16216
Library of Congress Control Number: 2015952351

Printed in the USA
For more Disney Press fun, visit www.disneybooks.com

Hapana! It's raining hard in the Pride Lands! The baboons are caught up in a tree.

In Swahili, "Hapana!" means "Oh, no!"

2

They will not come down.
Help, Lion Guard!

"Bunga, climb up and scare the baboons down!" says Kion.
"*Zuka Zama!*" Bunga shouts.

"*Zuka, zama!*" means "**Pop up, dive down!**" in Swahili.

PPFFFFTT!

He climbs up and makes a
loud noise.
It works! The Lion Guard
saves the baboons!

Kion goes to speak to Mufasa.
"The rains cause problems," Kion says.
"I could blow them away with my roar."

"The easy way is not always the best way," Mufasa says. "The rains are part of the Circle of Life."

Later the Lion Guard gets a wet surprise.
"There has never been a river here
before!" says Fuli.

Ono flies above to take a look.
"The lake is flooding!" he says.

Bunga has an idea.

He tells Beshte to push the rocks.

The rocks block the water.

Then Bunga sees a leak.
"Let's put a stick in it."
It works!

"That was quick and easy,"
Bunga says.

Kion remembers Mufasa's advice: *The easy way is not always the best way.*

Bunga hears Rafiki say, "Honey badgers are the smartest animals." Bunga runs to tell everyone.

But Rafiki was not done talking. "Honey badgers are the smartest when they think first."

The Lion Guard sees a lot of animals heading to Hakuna Matata Falls.

"Get in line to see Bunga the Wise!"
calls Timon.

"*Hevi kabisa!*" Kion says.
"What's going on?"

Bunga shrugs. "I can help everyone by telling them what to do."

In Swahili, "Hevi kabisa!" means **"Totally intense!"**

"Bunga should not give advice," says Fuli.

"He *did* figure out how to stop the flooding," Beshte says.

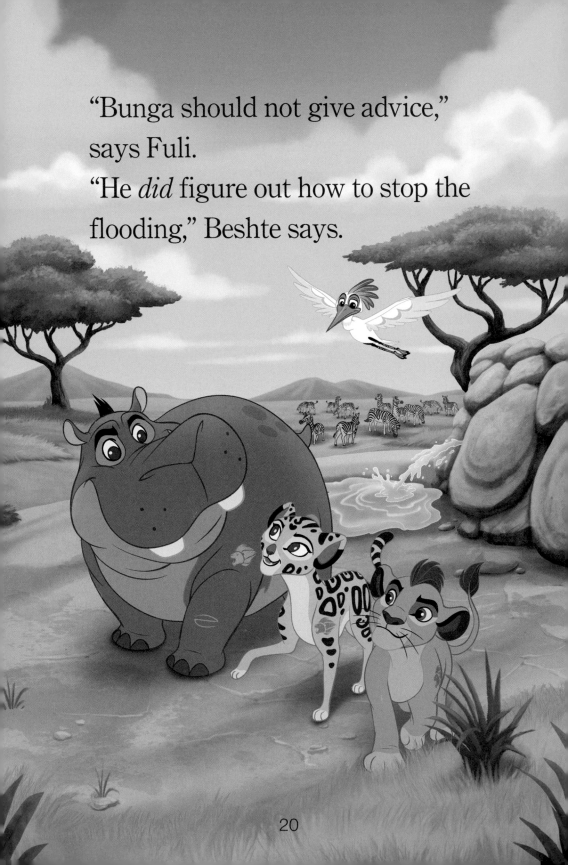

But everywhere they go, the Guard finds animals that need help.

An ostrich told Bunga she was scared to see hyenas.

So Bunga told her to bury her head.

Bad advice, Bunga.

Bunga told the bushbucks the pink
flowers were the tastiest.

"Wait!" says Beshte. "The pink flowers
will make you sick!"

"Bunga, your bad advice is making things worse!" says Kion.

Suddenly, the dam breaks!
"Run!" yells Timon.

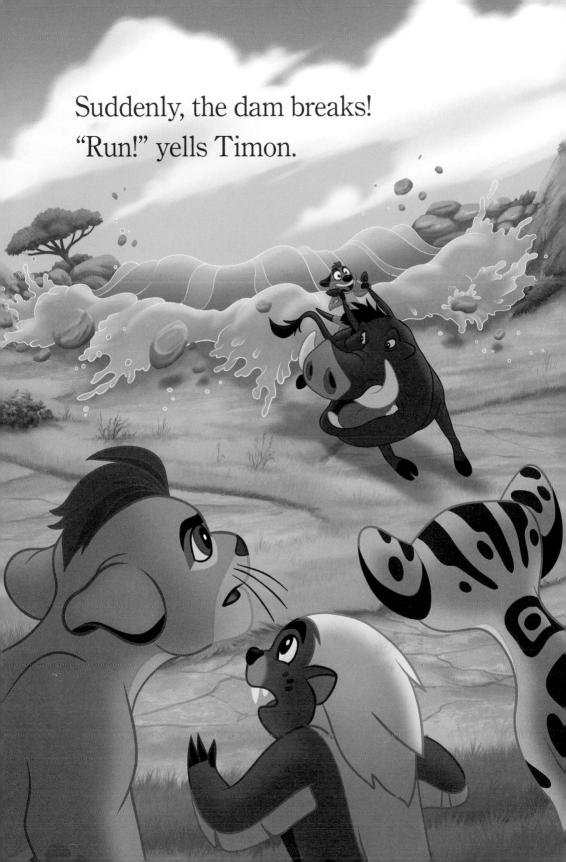

Kion leads the animals into the canyon. But the flood keeps coming.

The animals ask Bunga what to do.
"I don't know. Ask Kion!" Bunga says.

Kion has an idea. "Get behind me!"
He lets out a mighty roar!

Kion's roar stops the flood!

The animals in the Pride Lands
are safe.
Rafiki tells Bunga honey badgers
are the smartest . . .

when they think first.

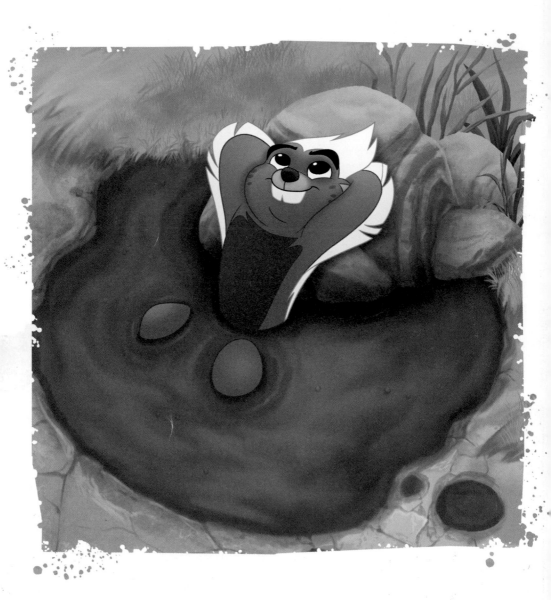

"I guess I'm not so wise after all," says Bunga. "I can live with that."